Willow
Tree

This edition published by Willow Tree Books, 2018
Willow Tree Books, Tide Mill Way, Woodbridge, Suffolk, IP12 1AP

0 2 4 6 8 9 7 5 3 1

Text © 2015 Helen Oswald
Illustration © 2015 Zoe Waring

Willow Tree Books and associated logos are trademarks and/or
registered trademarks of Tide Mill Media Ltd

Written by Helen Oswald
Illustrated by Zoe Waring

ISBN: 978-1-78700-455-9
Manufactured in China

www.willowtreebooks.net

CAT & DOG

Helen Oswald

Zoe Waring

Cat slept in the day.

Dog slept at night.

But every evening, as the sun went down,
they met for a scrap.

One such evening, Dog and Cat's scrap turned into a big argument...

"Is it true you cats can see in the dark?" asked Dog.

"Of course! I'm over here you silly dog," hissed Cat.

"Well, I don't believe you!" barked Dog.

"We are busy at night," said Cat.

"Silly Cat! Your life's all upside down!" said Dog.

"oh yes it is!"

Cat and Dog turned their backs on each other.
It was the biggest argument they'd ever had.

Evenings went by, and both
Dog and Cat stood their ground.

Dog only came out during the day...

and Cat only
came out
at night.

Deep down, Cat missed scrapping with Dog, and Dog missed fighting Cat...
but they were both too stubborn to say anything.

Finally, one day, Dog gave in and whispered,
"I'm sorry I said your life was all upside down, Cat. I miss you."

But Cat was fast asleep and didn't hear a thing.

One night, Cat gave in too and whispered, "I'm sorry I dropped an apple on your head, Dog. I miss you."

But Dog was fast asleep and didn't hear a thing.

"I have an idea how I can help Dog
stay awake ALL night," thought Cat, happily.

"I have an idea how I can help Cat stay
awake ALL day," thought Dog, wagging his tail.

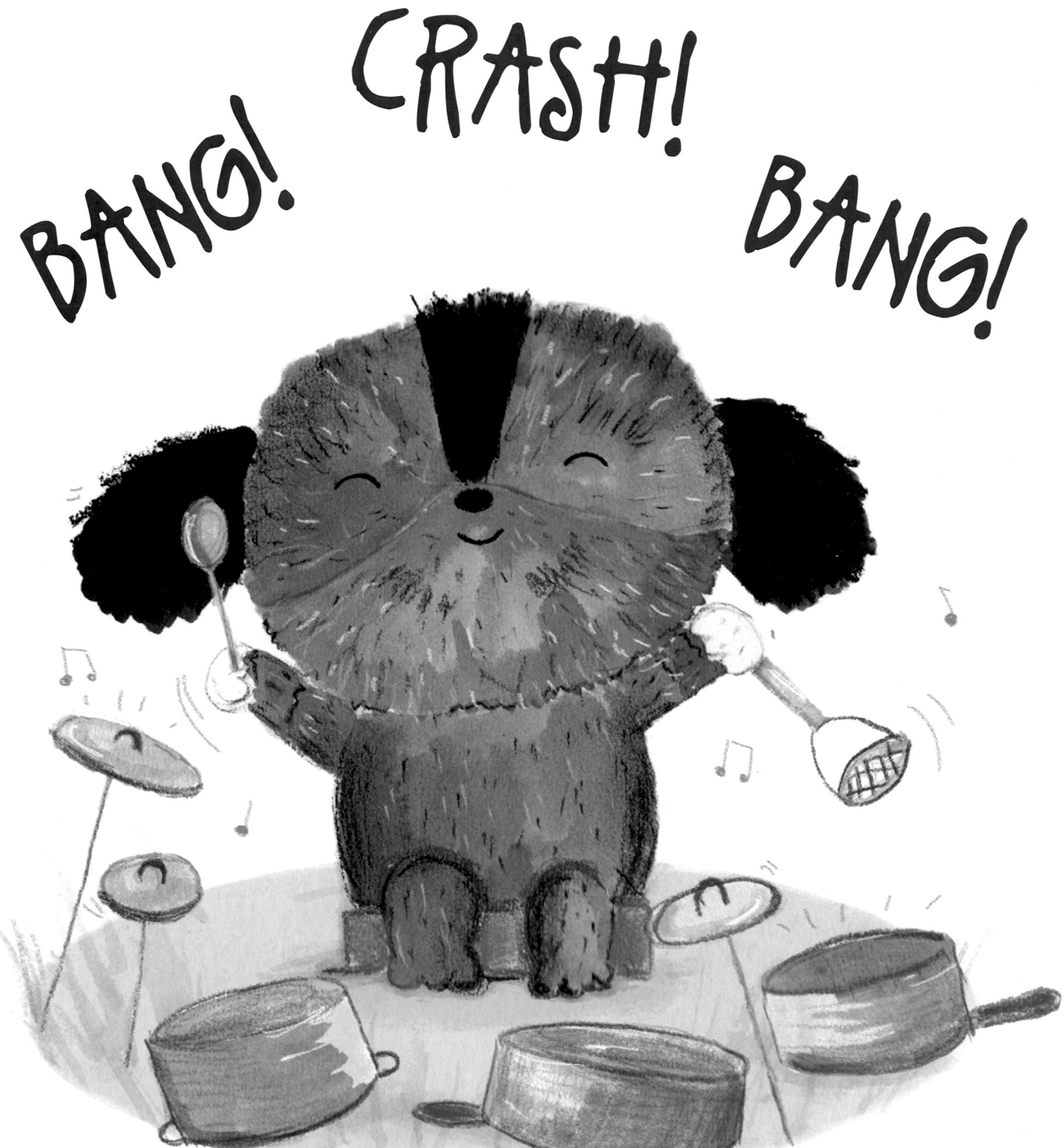
BANG!
CRASH!
BANG!

"What were you doing up there anyway?" asked Dog.

"Stringing up lights so you can see in the dark,
and we can scrap ALL night," answered Cat.

"What were you making that awful racket for?" asked Cat.

"To help you stay awake so we can fight ALL day," said Dog.

"You're barking mad!"

"Well, you're hardly purrrrrfect!
Let's be the best of enemies, and scrap forever!"

So, every evening from then on, the two friends scrapped happily ever after.